MOTHER GOOSE

MOTHER GOOSE

THE ORIGINAL
VOLLAND EDITION

Arranged and Edited by
EULALIE   OSGOOD   GROVER

Illustrated   by
FREDERICK   RICHARDSON

DERRYDALE BOOKS
New York

This edition is published by Derrydale Books,
a division of Random House Value Publishing, Inc.,
210 East 50th Street, New York, New York 10022.

Derrydale Books and colophon are trademarks of
Random House Value Publishing, Inc.

Random House
New York • Toronto • London • Sydney • Auckland
http://www.randomhouse.com/

Library of Congress Cataloging-in-Publication Data
Mother Goose.
Summary: Presents 108 illustrated Mother Goose rhymes including "Old Mother Hubbard" and "Goosey, goosey, gander."
1. Nursery rhymes. [1. Nursery rhymes]. I. Grover, Eulalie Osgood, 1873-
II. Richardson, Frederick, 1862-1937, ill. III. Title.
PZ8.3.M85Gro 1984 398'.8 83-23939
ISBN: 0-517-43619-1

27 26 25 24

Dedicated by the
Compiler *and* Artist
to
VIRGINIA *and* DORIS
and their mother,
the inspiration of the publisher

PREFACE

It is a great pleasure to see the republication of this beautiful edition of Mother Goose rhymes. The popularity of these rhymes is at least as strong today as it was when this book was first published almost seventy years ago. Of Mother Goose, Eulalie Osgood Grover says in her Foreword to the 1915 edition, "May her fame and her melodies be lovingly preserved to give joy and inspiration to many future generations of little children."

And there has never been more a loving preservation than this book. Much care has been taken to faithfully reproduce Frederick Richardson's exquisite color illustrations, which accompany the well-known rhymes so beautifully. The binding is Smythe-sewn to ensure sturdiness and a long life. In all, this book is meant to be an enduring family treasure, to be enjoyed by all and to hold a cherished place on the bookshelf.

COREY NASH

New York City

A FOREWORD

Children, as well as their interested parents, will eagerly welcome this beautiful edition of the one great nursery classic, just as a worthy edition of Shakespeare is welcomed by discriminating adult readers.

But some may ask what there is in these simple melodies, attributed to Mother Goose, which gives them so secure and beloved a place in the home, the school and the public library. Is it the humor, the action, the rhythm, or the mystery of the theme which appeals so strongly to critical little minds in each generation of childhood, and even to adult minds so fortunate as to have retained some of the refreshing naiveté of early years?

It is useless to try to explain the charm of these nonsense melodies. The children themselves do not know why they love them. No mother can tell us the magic of the spell which seems to be cast over her restless baby as she croons to it a Mother Goose lullaby. No primary teacher quite understands why the mere repetition or singing of a Mother Goose jingle will transform her listless, inattentive class into one all eagerness and attention. But mother and teacher agree that the best of these verses have an even more potent influence than that of innocently diverting and entertaining the child. The healthy moral, so subtly suggested in many of the rhymes, is unconsciously absorbed by the child's receptive mind, helping him to make his own distinction between right and wrong, bravery and cowardice, generosity and selfishness.

From a literary standpoint, also, these rhymes have proved of real value in creating a taste for the truly musical in poetry and song. They train the ear and stir the imagination of the child as no other verses do. Many famous poets and writers trace their first inspiration, and love for things literary, back to the nursery songs and fairy tales of their childhood.

Teachers well know that children who have reveled in these rhymes and stories, at the time of their strongest appeal, step naturally and appreciatively into the great fields of good literature which are beyond.

Knowing these things to be true, we do not hesitate to place this venerable classic on the shelf beside our Shakespeare, and to send our children there for delight and inspiration. They will understand Shakespeare the better for having known and loved Mother Goose.

But what about the personality of this classic writer? Was she really Mistress Elizabeth Goose who is said to have lived in Boston about two hundred years ago, and who crooned her nonsense jingles to a large and happy family of grandchildren? We are told that their father, Thomas Fleet, who was a printer by trade, thought to turn an honest penny with his mother-in-law's popular verses, so he published them in a small volume under the title of "Songs for the Nursery: or, Mother Goose's Melodies." A goose with a very long neck and a wide-open mouth flew across the title page, at least so the story goes. But we have to believe that it is only a story, for no copy of the book can be found, and nothing but tradition identifies Elizabeth Goose, the Boston grandmother, with the famous rhymester.

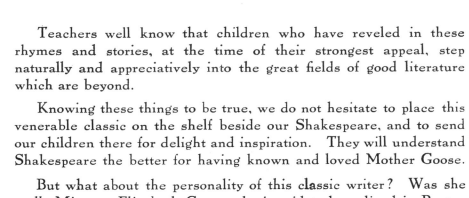

We might feel sorry to be obliged to discredit this picturesque story of Mother Goose, if her real history were not even more mysterious. We know very little about the beloved patron of childhood, but what we do know is as follows:

Mother Goose is most certainly of respectable French origin, for in 1697 a distinguished French writer, Charles Perrault, published in Paris a little book of familiar stories called "Contes de ma Mère l'Oye," or "Tales of My Mother Goose." Her identity, however, he leaves a mystery, except that in the frontispiece of his book is pictured an old woman by her fireside telling stories to an eager little family group.

This volume contained the only prose tales that have ever been credited to Mother Goose, and they are still among the most popular stories in nursery or school room. The titles are as follows: "Little Red Riding Hood;" "The Sisters Who Dropped From Their Mouths Diamonds and Toads;" "Bluebeard;" "The Sleeping Beauty;" "Puss in Boots;" "Cinderella;" "Riquet With the Tuft;" and "Tom Thumb."

It is through her verses, however, that Mother Goose has won her well-deserved fame. The first collection under her name was published in London about 1765 by John Newbery. It may be, if Oliver Goldsmith were living, he could tell us more about the origin of these verses than we are now ever likely to know. It is more than probable that he himself edited the little volume for John Newbery, and that he wrote the clever preface, "By a very Great Writer of very Little Books," as well as the quaint moral which supplements each rhyme.

About twenty-five years later this book was reprinted in our country by Isaiah Thomas of Worcester, Massachusetts. Several copies of this edition are preserved, one of which has been photographed and reproduced in facsimile by W. H. Whitmore of Boston. Other publishers also reprinted the English edition, one being done for John Newbery's grandson, Francis Power, in 1791.

In 1810 another collection of melodies appeared under the title of "Gammer Gurton's Garland." It was quite evidently a rival of Mother Goose, though it contained nearly all of her verses, besides many far less interesting ones gathered from other sources.

Gammer Gurton's popularity, however, was short, and Mother Goose was revived about 1825 by a Boston firm, Munroe and Francis. Since that time her fame has never waned. In spite of the present multiplicity of beautiful books for children, they are constantly exhausting large editions of the one universally beloved book of melodies. Some of these volumes have been collected and edited by men of the highest literary judgment and ability, such as Goldsmith (with hardly a doubt), Ritson, Halliwell, Andrew Lang, Charles Eliot Norton, Charles Welsh and Edward Everett Hale. Certainly there is not another collection of juvenile literature which can boast such a list of scholarly editors. The deepest gratitude is due them for their careful and discriminating effort to preserve for the children of future generations this rich heritage of nursery melodies.

Many less discriminating editors, however, have ruthlessly mutilated and adapted many of the rhymes to suit their fancy, thinking, possibly, that as Mother Goose is only a title, the verses attributed to her belong to the general public to use as it sees fit. On the contrary, Mother Goose's melodies belong to the children, and no addition or change should be made except by those who are in such close sympathy with the child-heart that they may act with the child's authority.

This present edition of "Mother Goose" preserves the best of the verses which became so popular in England and America as to first demand their publication. It is the only truly classic edition that has been published in modern times. The two authorities which have been followed are the edition published for John Newbery's grandson in London in 1791, and probably edited by Oliver Goldsmith, and the edition published in Boston in 1833 by Munroe and Francis, called "The Only True Mother Goose Melodies." It is from this copy that the following quaint introduction by "Ma'am Goose" is quoted.

Not all the favorites among the nursery rhymes are here, only those that first helped to make the fame of the fictitious but no less worthy patron of childhood. May her fame and her melodies be lovingly preserved to give joy and inspiration to many future generations of little children.

EULALIE OSGOOD GROVER

1915

Hear What Ma'am Goose Says!

My dear little Blossoms, there are now in this world, and always will be, a great many grannies beside myself, both in petticoats and pantaloons, some a deal younger, to be sure, but all monstrous wise and of my own family name. These old women, who never had chick or child of their own, but who always know how to bring up other people's children, will tell you with long faces that my enchanting, quieting, soothing volume, my all-sufficient anodyne for cross, peevish, won't-be-comforted little bairns, ought be laid aside for more learned books, such as *they* could select and publish. Fudge! I tell you that all their batterings can't deface my beauties, nor their wise pratings equal my wiser prattlings; and all imitators of my refreshing songs might as well write another Billy Shakespeare as another Mother Goose—we two great poets were born together, and shall go out of the world together.

> No, no, my melodies will never die,
> While nurses sing, or babies cry.

From "The Only True Mother Goose Melodies,"
Published by Munroe & Francis, Boston, 1833

MOTHER GOOSE

Old Mother Goose, when
She wanted to wander,
Would ride through the air
On a very fine gander.

Cock-a-doodle-doo,
My dame has lost her shoe:
My master's lost his fiddlestick,
And knows not what to do.

Peter, Peter, pumpkin eater,
Had a wife and couldn't keep her;
He put her in a pumpkin shell,
And then he kept her very well.

Peter, Peter, pumpkin eater,
Had another, and didn't love her;
Peter learned to read and spell,
And then he loved her very well.

Lady-bird, Lady-bird,
Fly away home,
Your house is on fire,
Your children will burn.

One misty, moisty morning,
  When cloudy was the weather,
I chanced to meet an old man clothed all in leather.
He began to compliment, and I began to grin,
  How do you do, and how do you do?
  And how do you do again?

I like little pussy, her coat is so warm,
And if I don't hurt her she'll do me no harm;
So I'll not pull her tail, nor drive her away,
But pussy and I very gently will play.

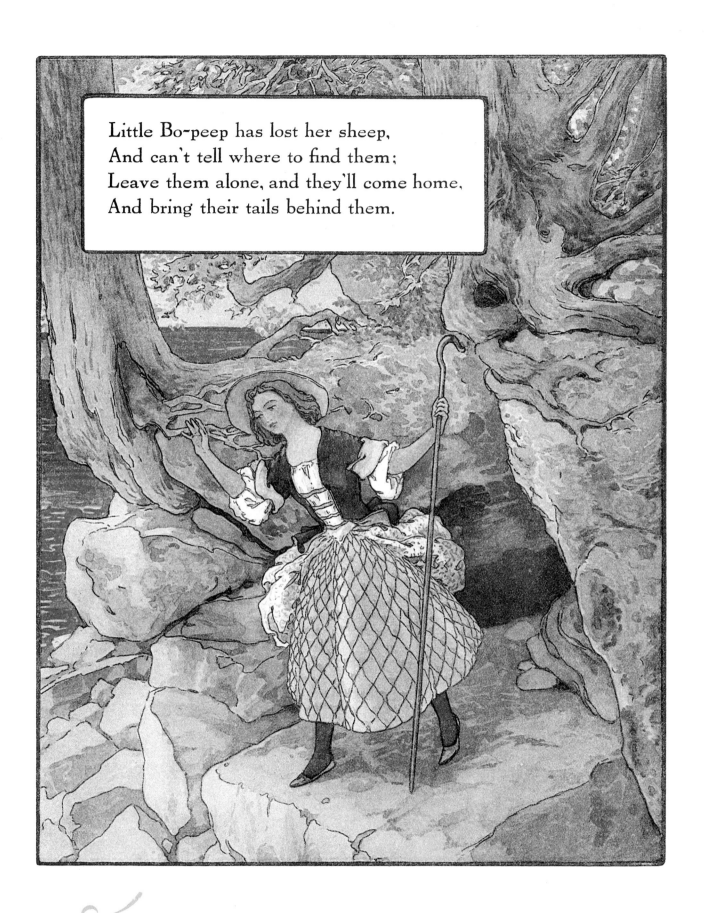

Little Bo-peep has lost her sheep,
And can't tell where to find them;
Leave them alone, and they'll come home,
And bring their tails behind them.

Little Nanny Etticoat
In a white petticoat,
   And a red nose;
The longer she stands
   The shorter she grows.

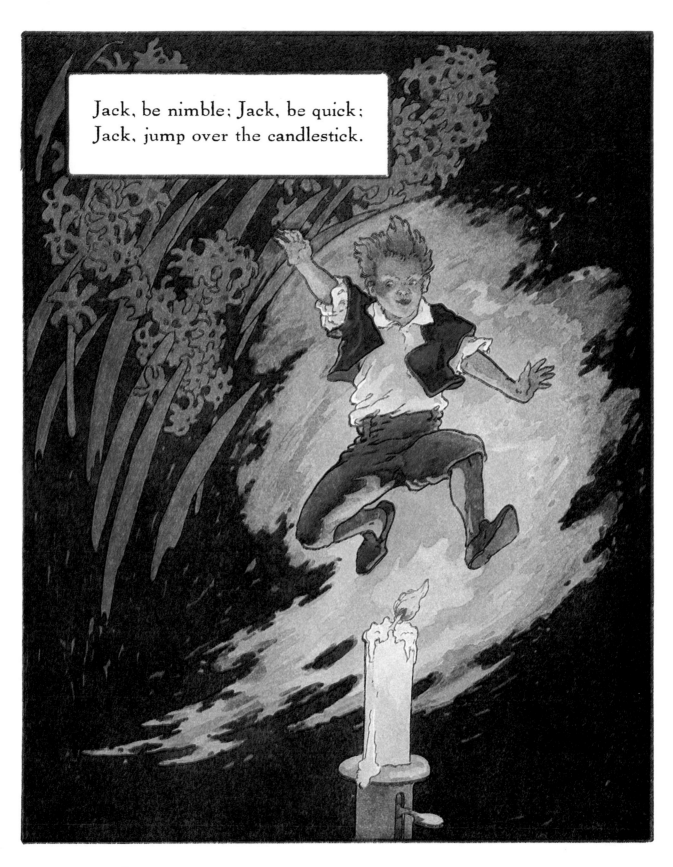

Jack, be nimble; Jack, be quick;
Jack, jump over the candlestick.

Pretty John Watts,
We are troubled with rats.
Will you drive them out of the house?
We have mice, too, in plenty,
That feast in the pantry,
But let them stay
And nibble away,
What harm in a little brown mouse?

I'll tell you a story
About Mary Morey,
And now my story's begun.
I'll tell you another
About her brother,
And now my story's done.

Hush-a-bye, Baby, upon the tree top,
When the wind blows the cradle will rock;
When the bough breaks the cradle will fall,
Down tumbles cradle and Baby and all.

Ride away, ride away,
   Johnny shall ride,
And he shall have pussy-cat
   Tied to one side;
And he shall have little dog
   Tied to the other,
And Johnny shall ride
   To see his grandmother.

Dickery, dickery, dock,
The mouse ran up the clock;
The clock struck one,
The mouse ran down,
Dickery, dickery, dock.

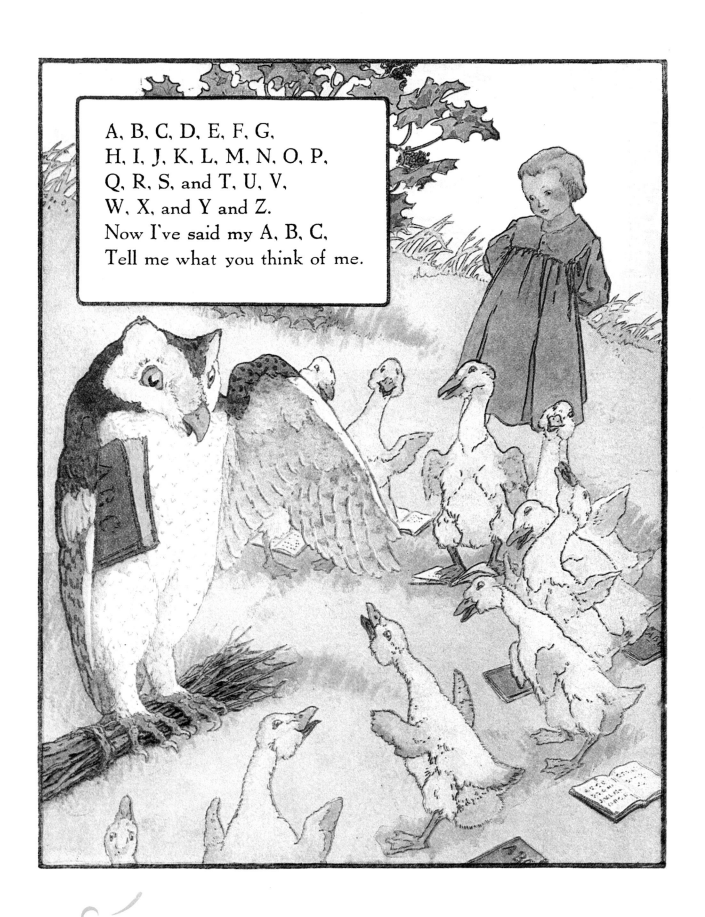

A, B, C, D, E, F, G,
H, I, J, K, L, M, N, O, P,
Q, R, S, and T, U, V,
W, X, and Y and Z.
Now I've said my A, B, C,
Tell me what you think of me.

The little robin grieves
    When the snow is on the ground,
For the trees have no leaves,
    And no berries can be found.

The air is cold, the worms are hid;
    For robin here what can be done?
Let's strow around some crumbs of bread,
    And then he'll live till snow is gone.

Little Tommy Tittlemouse
Lived in a little house;
He caught fishes
In other men's ditches.

About the bush, Willie, about the bee-hive,
About the bush, Willie, I'll meet thee alive.

Bah, bah, black sheep,
　　Have you any wool?
Yes, marry, have I,
　　Three bags full;
One for my master,
　　One for my dame,
But none for the little boy
　　Who cries in the lane.

Hickety, pickety, my black hen,
She lays eggs for gentlemen:
Gentlemen come every day
To see what my black hen doth lay.

Willie boy, Willie boy,
  Where are you going?
O, let us go with you
  This sunshiny day.

I'm going to the meadow
  To see them a-mowing,
I'm going to help the girls
  Turn the new hay.

Three children sliding on the ice
    Upon a summer's day,
As it fell out, they all fell in,
    The rest they ran away.

Oh, had these children been at school,
    Or sliding on dry ground,
Ten thousand pounds to one penny
    They had not then been drowned.

Ye parents who have children dear,
    And ye, too, who have none,
If you would keep them safe abroad,
    Pray keep them safe at home.

Wee Willie Winkie runs through the town,
Upstairs and downstairs, in his nightgown;
Tapping at the window, crying at the lock:
"Are the babes in their beds, for it's now ten o'clock?

There was an old woman who lived in a shoe,
She had so many children she didn't know what to do.
She gave them some broth without any bread,
She whipped them all soundly and put them to bed.

There was a man and he had naught,
    And robbers came to rob him;
He crept up to the chimney top,
    And then they thought they had him.
But he got down on the other side,
    And then they could not find him;
He ran fourteen miles in fifteen days,
    And never looked behind him.

There was an old man,
And he had a calf,
And that's half;
He took him out of the stall,
And put him on the wall,
And that's all.

Bow, wow, wow!
Whose dog art thou?
Little Tom Tinker's dog,
Bow, wow, wow!

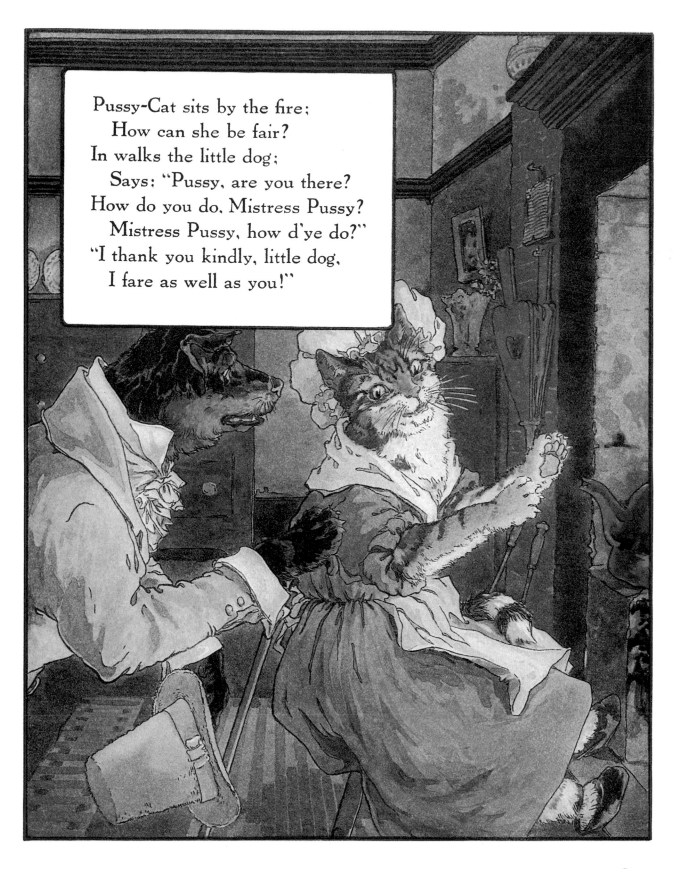

Pussy-Cat sits by the fire;
   How can she be fair?
In walks the little dog;
   Says: "Pussy, are you there?
How do you do, Mistress Pussy?
   Mistress Pussy, how d'ye do?"
"I thank you kindly, little dog,
   I fare as well as you!"

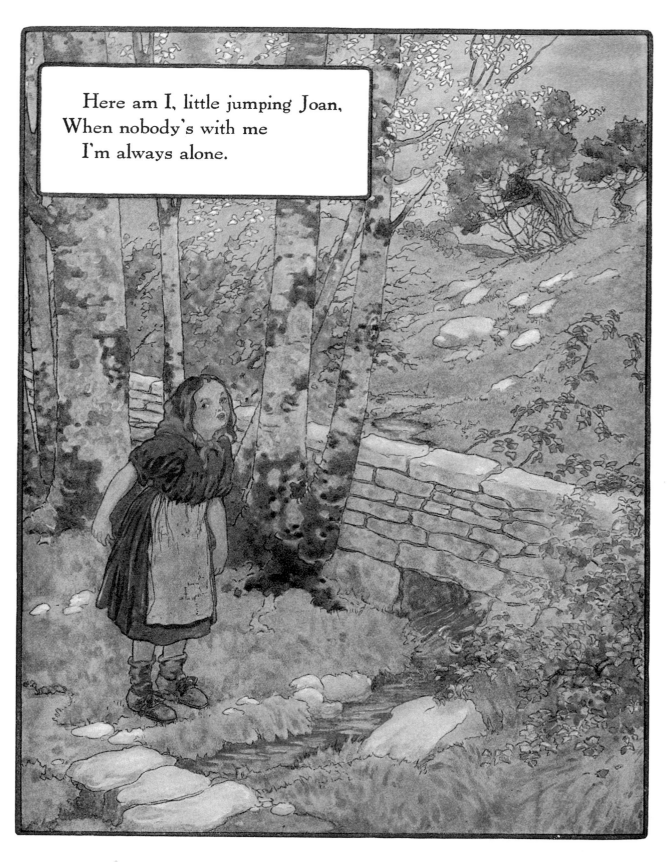

Here am I, little jumping Joan,
When nobody's with me
I'm always alone.

There was an old woman lived under the hill,
And if she's not gone she lives there still.
Baked apples she sold, and cranberry pies,
And she's the old woman that never told lies.

Simple Simon met a pieman
　　Going to the fair;
Says Simple Simon to the pieman:
　"Pray let me taste your ware."

Says the pieman to Simple Simon:
　"Show me first your penny;"
Says Simple Simon to the pieman:
　"Indeed I have not any."

Sing a song of sixpence, a bag full of rye,
Four and twenty blackbirds baked in a pie;
When the pie was opened the birds began to sing,
And wasn't this a dainty dish to set before the king?
The king was in the parlor counting out his money;
The queen was in the kitchen eating bread and honey;
The maid was in the garden hanging out the clothes,
There came a little blackbird and nipped off her nose.

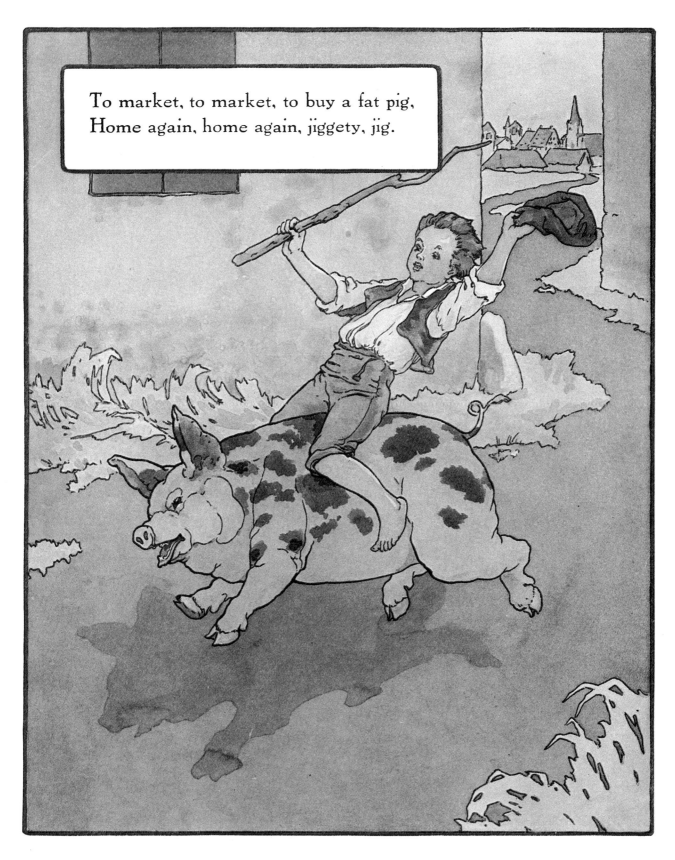

To market, to market, to buy a fat pig,
Home again, home again, jiggety, jig.

Ride a cock horse
To Banbury Cross
To see what Tommy can buy:
A penny white loaf,
A penny white cake,
And a two-penny apple pie.

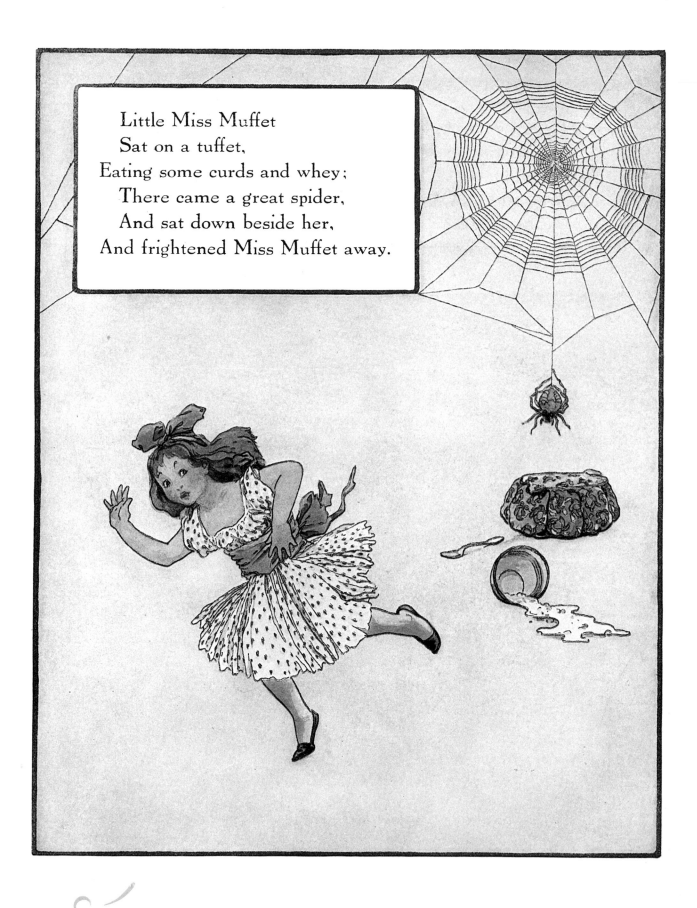

Little Miss Muffet
Sat on a tuffet,
Eating some curds and whey;
There came a great spider,
And sat down beside her,
And frightened Miss Muffet away.

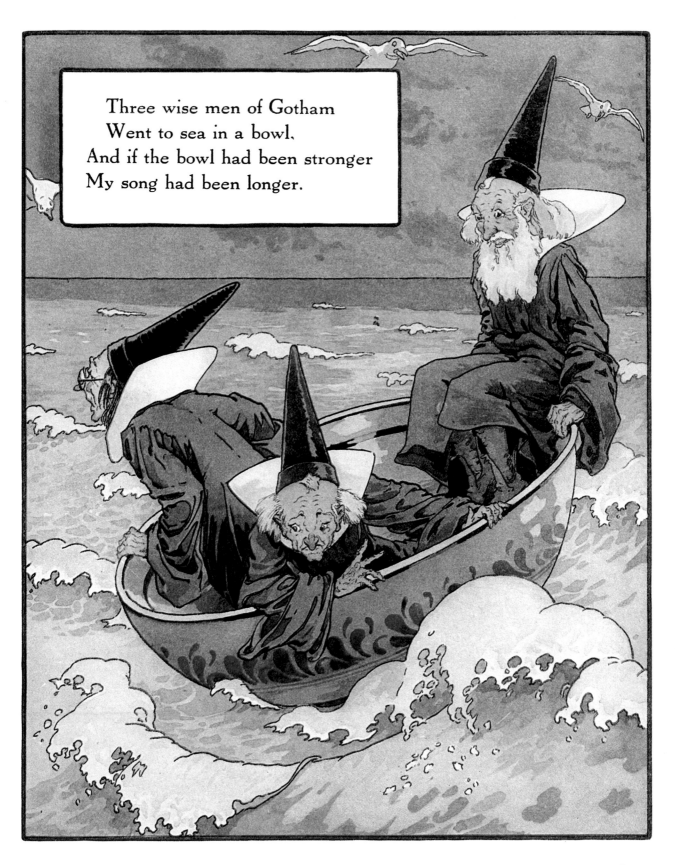

Three wise men of Gotham
Went to sea in a bowl,
And if the bowl had been stronger
My song had been longer.

There were two birds sat upon a stone,
    Fal de ral—al de ral—laddy.
One flew away and then there was one,
    Fal de ral—al de ral—laddy.
The other flew after and then there was none,
    Fal de ral—al de ral—laddy.
So the poor stone was left all alone,
    Fal de ral—al de ral—laddy.
One of these little birds back again flew,
    Fal de ral—al de ral—laddy.
The other came after and then there were two,
    Fal de ral—al de ral—laddy.
Says one to the other: "Pray, how do you do?"
    Fal de ral—al de ral—laddy.
"Very well, thank you, and pray how are you?"
    Fal de ral—al de ral—laddy.

Bye, Baby bunting,
Father's gone a-hunting,
Mother's gone a-milking,
Sister's gone a-silking,
And Brother's gone to buy a skin
To wrap the Baby bunting in.

Little Polly Flinders
Sat among the cinders
      Warming her pretty little toes;
Her mother came and caught her,
Whipped her little daughter
      For spoiling her nice new clothes.

Tom, Tom, the piper's son,
Stole a pig, and away he run;
   The pig was eat,
    And Tom was beat,
And Tom ran crying down the street.

Jack and Jill went up the hill
  To fetch a pail of water;
Jack fell down and broke his crown,
  And Jill came tumbling after.

A dillar, a dollar,
    A ten o'clock scholar;
What makes you come so soon?
    You used to come at ten o'clock,
But now you come at noon!

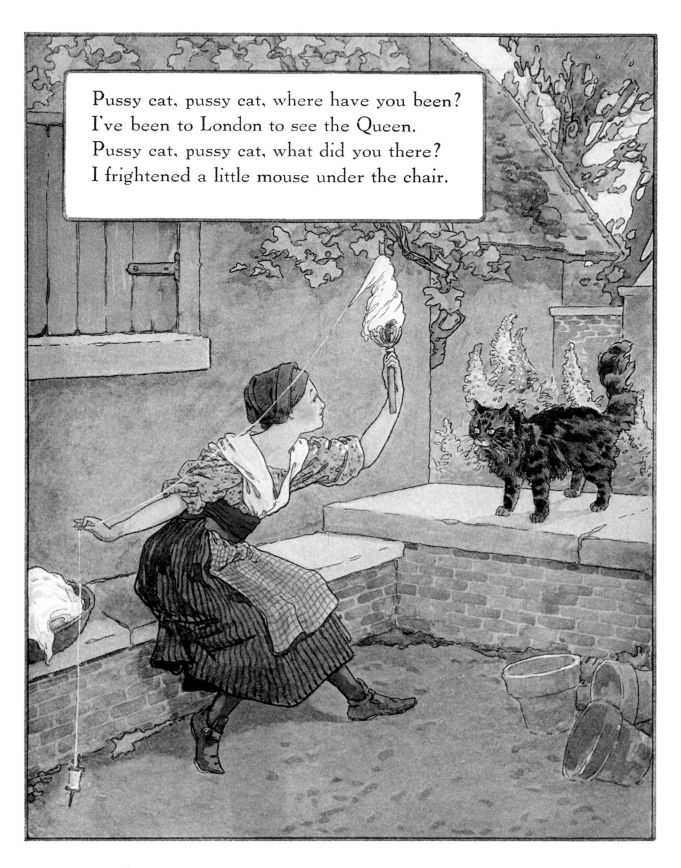

Pussy cat, pussy cat, where have you been?
I've been to London to see the Queen.
Pussy cat, pussy cat, what did you there?
I frightened a little mouse under the chair.

Pat a cake, pat a cake, Baker's man;
So I do, master, as fast as I can.
Pat it and prick it and mark it with T,
And then it will serve for Tommy and me.

Little Boy Blue, come blow your horn,
The sheep's in the meadow, the cow's in the corn.
What! Is this the way you mind your sheep,
Under the haycock fast asleep?

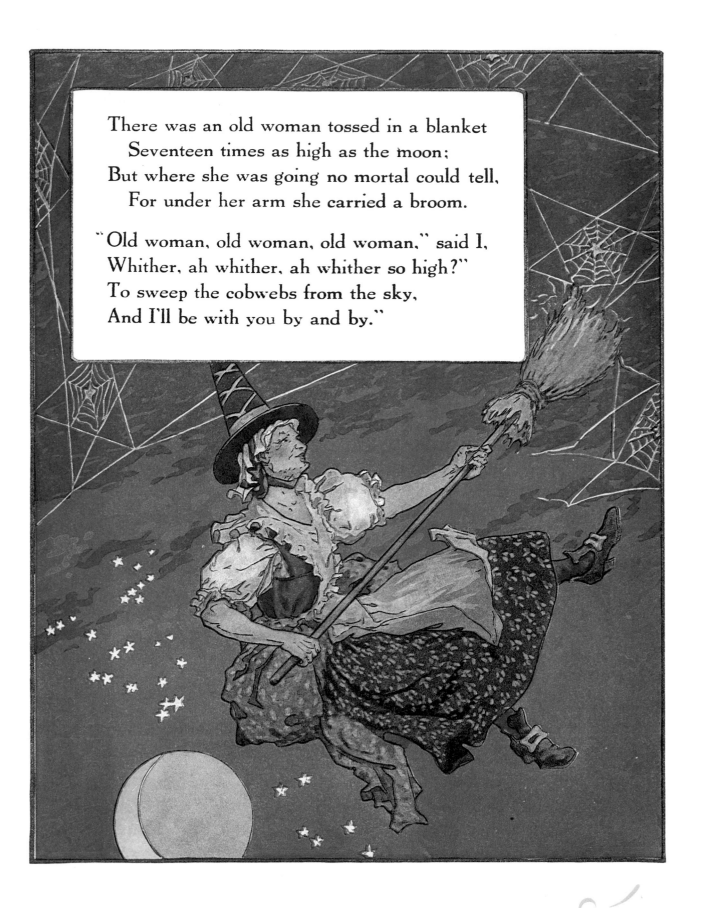

There was an old woman tossed in a blanket
  Seventeen times as high as the moon;
But where she was going no mortal could tell,
  For under her arm she carried a broom.

"Old woman, old woman, old woman," said I,
Whither, ah whither, ah whither so high?"
To sweep the cobwebs from the sky,
And I'll be with you by and by."

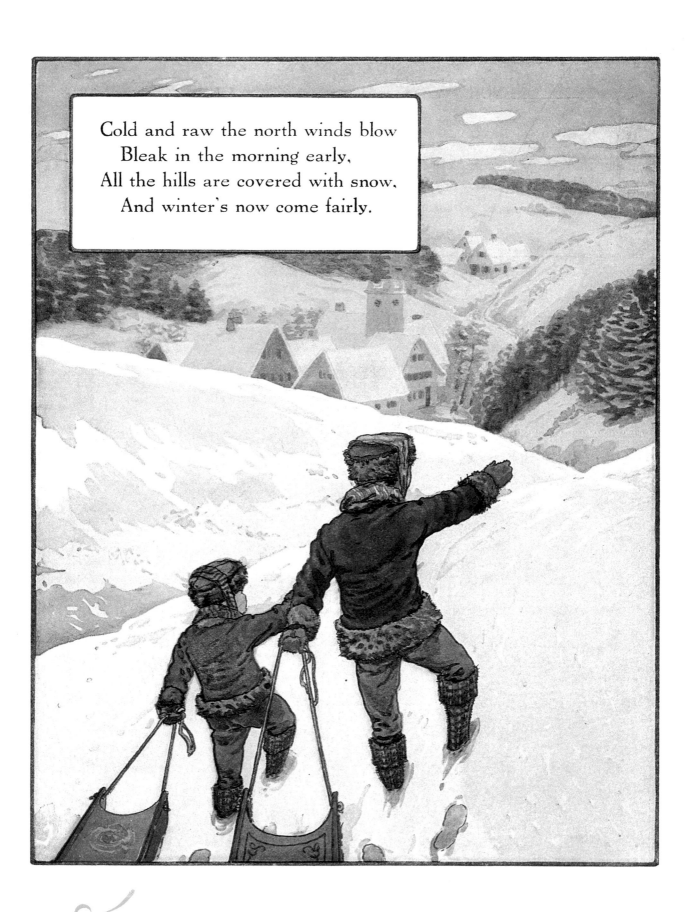

Cold and raw the north winds blow
Bleak in the morning early,
All the hills are covered with snow,
And winter's now come fairly.

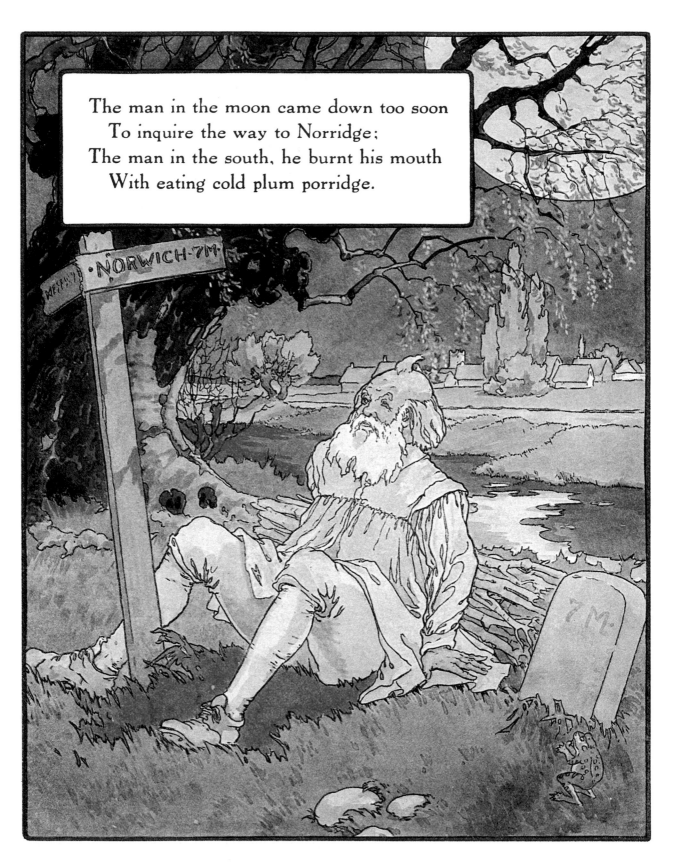

The man in the moon came down too soon
  To inquire the way to Norridge;
The man in the south, he burnt his mouth
  With eating cold plum porridge.

Four-and-twenty tailors
　　Went to kill a snail;
The best man among them
　　Durst not touch her tail;
She put out her horns
　　Like a little Kyloe cow.
Run, tailors, run, or
　　She'll kill you all just now.

Lucy Locket lost her pocket,
Kitty Fisher found it;
There was not a penny in it,
But a ribbon round it.

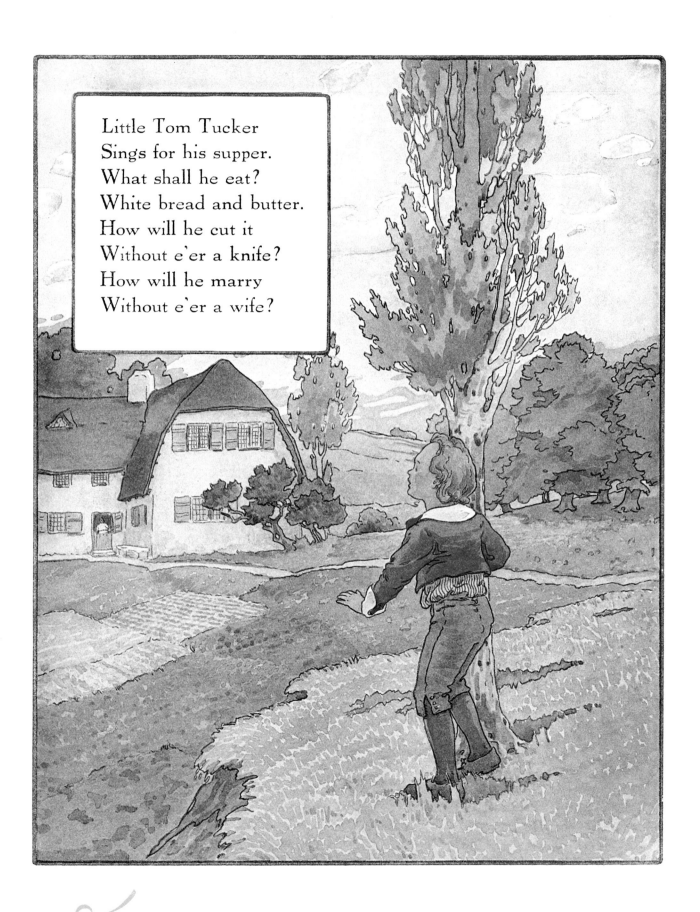

Little Tom Tucker
Sings for his supper.
What shall he eat?
White bread and butter.
How will he cut it
Without e'er a knife?
How will he marry
Without e'er a wife?

"To bed, to bed," says Sleepy-Head;
  "Let's stay awhile," says Slow;
"Put on the pot," says Greedy-Sot,
  "We'll sup before we go."

Diddle, diddle, dumpling, my son John,
Went to bed with his breeches on,
One stocking off, and one stocking on,
Diddle, diddle, dumpling, my son John.

High diddle diddle,
The cat and the fiddle,
The cow jumped over the moon;
The little dog laughed
To see such craft,
And the dish ran away with the spoon.

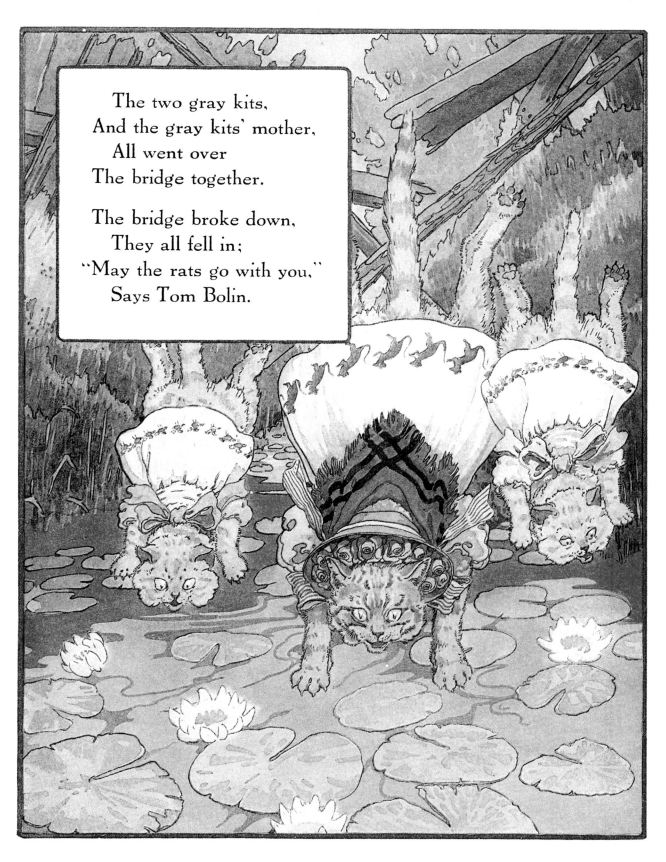

The two gray kits,
And the gray kits' mother,
All went over
The bridge together.

The bridge broke down,
They all fell in;
"May the rats go with you,"
Says Tom Bolin.

Robin and Richard
    Were two pretty men;
They stayed in bed
    Till the clock struck ten.
Then up starts Robin
    And looks at the sky:
"Oh, brother Richard,
    The sun's very high.
You go before
    With the bottle and bag,
And I will come after
    On little Jack nag."

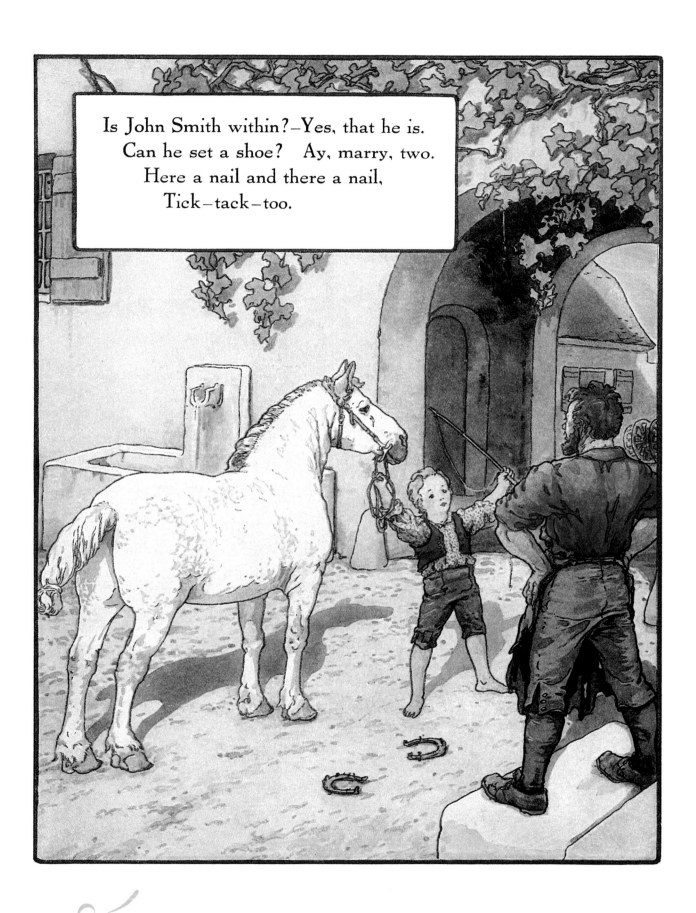

Is John Smith within?—Yes, that he is.
Can he set a shoe?   Ay, marry, two.
Here a nail and there a nail,
Tick–tack–too.

I had a little hen, the prettiest ever seen,
She washed me the dishes and kept the house clean.
She went to the mill to fetch me some flour,
And always got home in less than an hour.
She baked me my bread, she brewed me my ale,
She sat by the fire and told many a fine tale.

When I was a little boy I lived by myself,
And all the bread and cheese I got I put upon a shelf;
The rats and the mice, they made such a strife,
I was forced to go to London to buy me a wife.
The streets were so broad and the lanes were so narrow,
I was forced to bring my wife home in a wheelbarrow;
The wheelbarrow broke and my wife had a fall,
And down came the wheelbarrow, wife and all.

'Twas once upon a time, when Jenny Wren was young,
So daintily she danced and so prettily she sung,
Robin Redbreast lost his heart, for he was a gallant bird,
So he doffed his hat to Jenny Wren, requesting to be heard.

"O, dearest Jenny Wren, if you will but be mine,
You shall feed on cherry pie and drink new currant wine,
I'll dress you like a goldfinch or any peacock gay,
So, dearest Jen, if you'll be mine let us appoint the day."

Jenny blushed behind her fan and thus declared her mind:
"Since, dearest Bob, I love you well, I take your offer kind;
Cherry pie is very nice and so is currant wine,
But I must wear my plain brown gown and never go too fine."

How many days has my baby to play?
  Saturday, Sunday, Monday,
  Tuesday, Wednesday, Thursday, Friday,
  Saturday, Sunday, Monday.

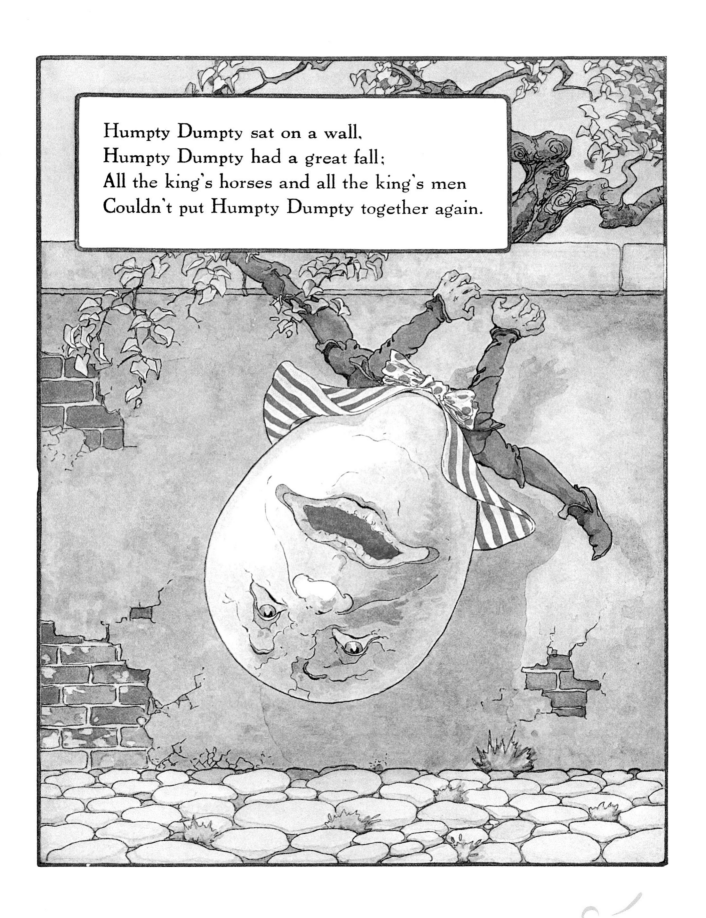

Humpty Dumpty sat on a wall,
Humpty Dumpty had a great fall;
All the king's horses and all the king's men
Couldn't put Humpty Dumpty together again.

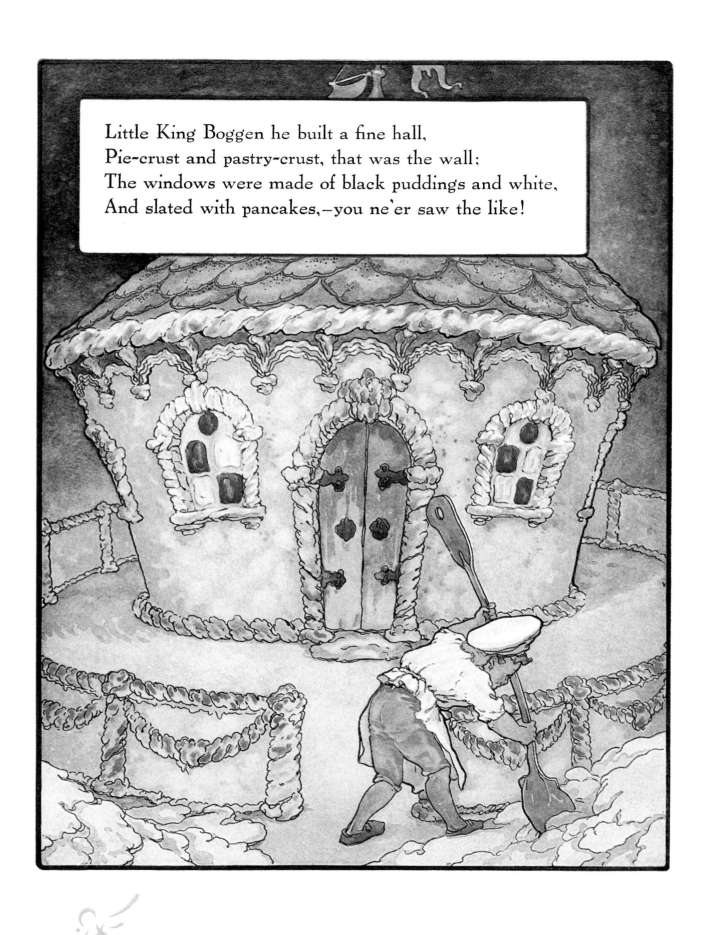

Little King Boggen he built a fine hall,
Pie-crust and pastry-crust, that was the wall;
The windows were made of black puddings and white,
And slated with pancakes,—you ne'er saw the like!

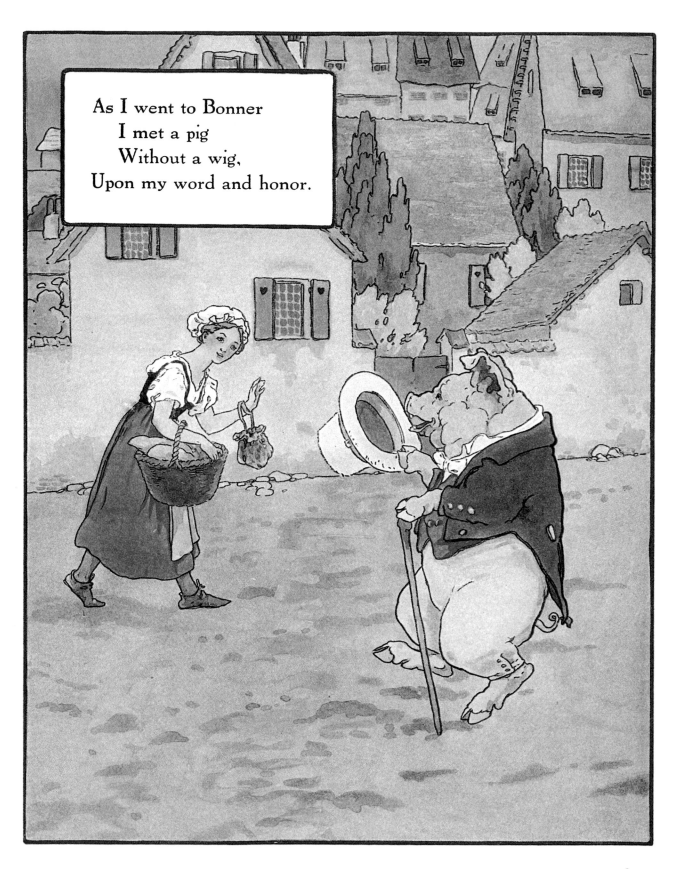

As I went to Bonner
    I met a pig
    Without a wig,
Upon my word and honor.

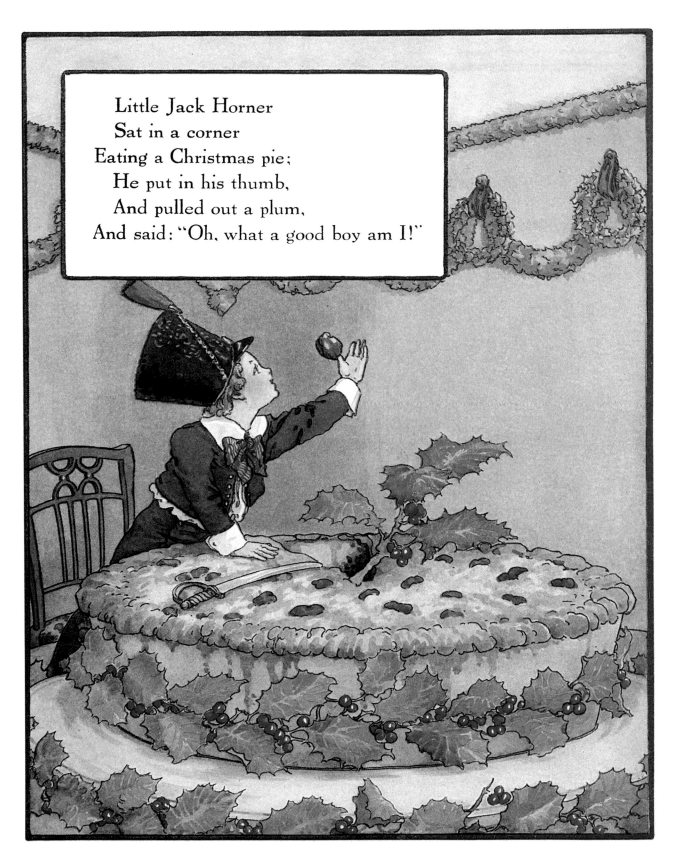

Little Jack Horner
  Sat in a corner
Eating a Christmas pie;
  He put in his thumb,
  And pulled out a plum,
And said: "Oh, what a good boy am I!"

Miss Jane had a bag and a mouse was in it;
She opened the bag, he was out in a minute.
The cat saw him jump and run under the table,
And the dog said: "Catch him, Puss, soon as you're able."

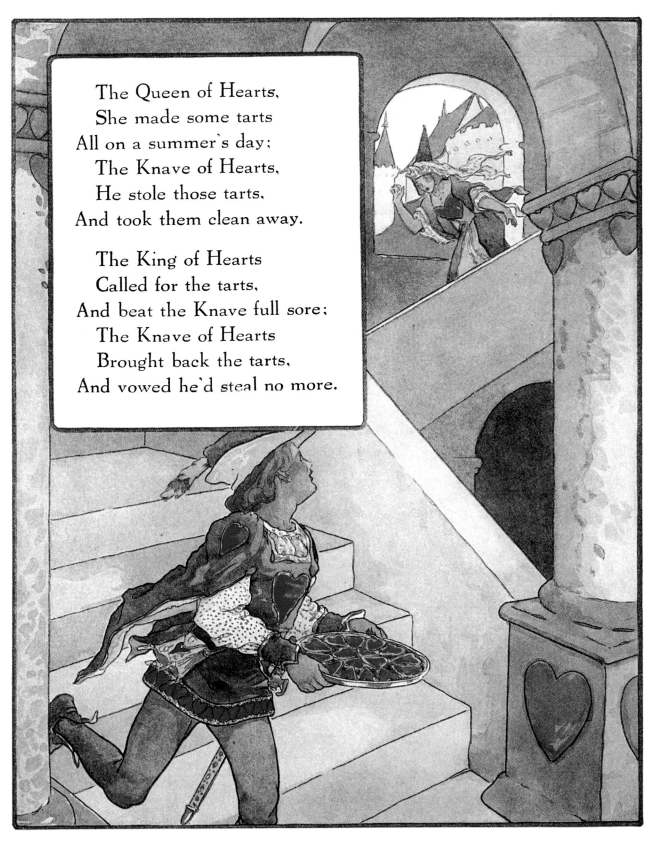

The Queen of Hearts,
She made some tarts
All on a summer's day;
The Knave of Hearts,
He stole those tarts,
And took them clean away.

The King of Hearts
Called for the tarts,
And beat the Knave full sore;
The Knave of Hearts
Brought back the tarts,
And vowed he'd steal no more.

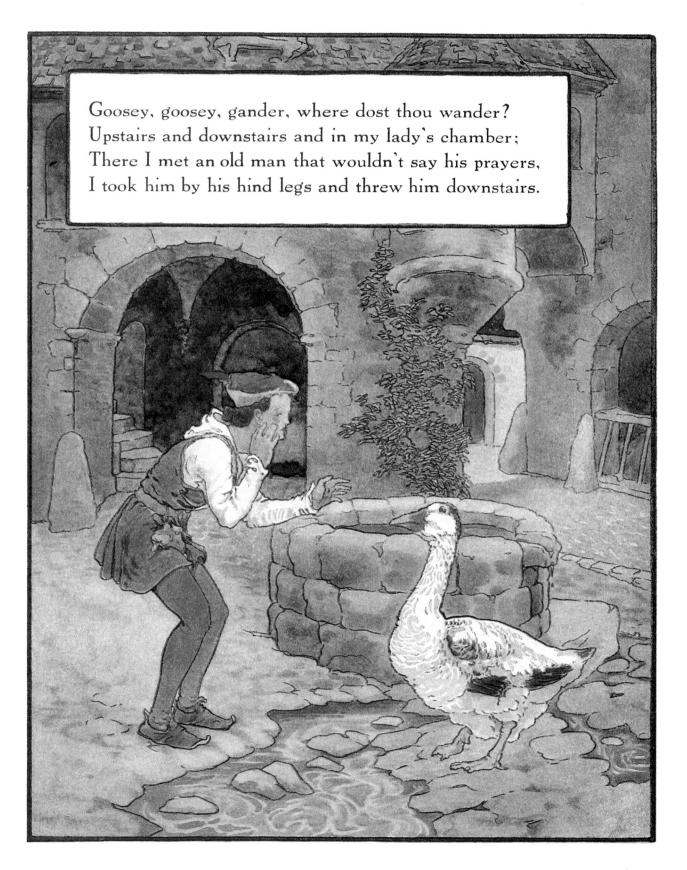

Goosey, goosey, gander, where dost thou wander?
Upstairs and downstairs and in my lady's chamber;
There I met an old man that wouldn't say his prayers,
I took him by his hind legs and threw him downstairs.

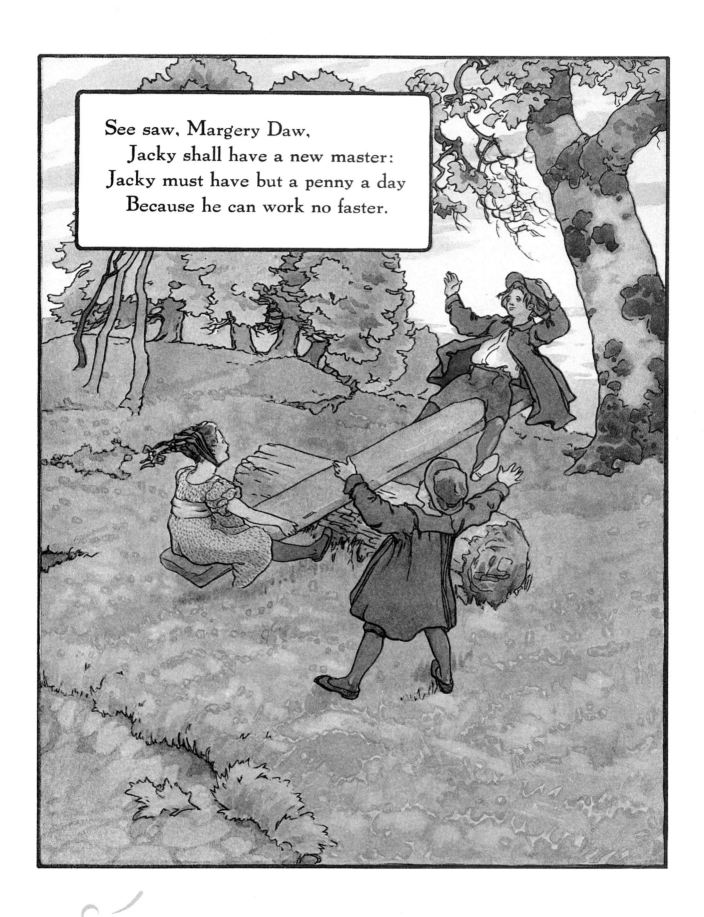

See saw, Margery Daw,
    Jacky shall have a new master:
Jacky must have but a penny a day
Because he can work no faster.

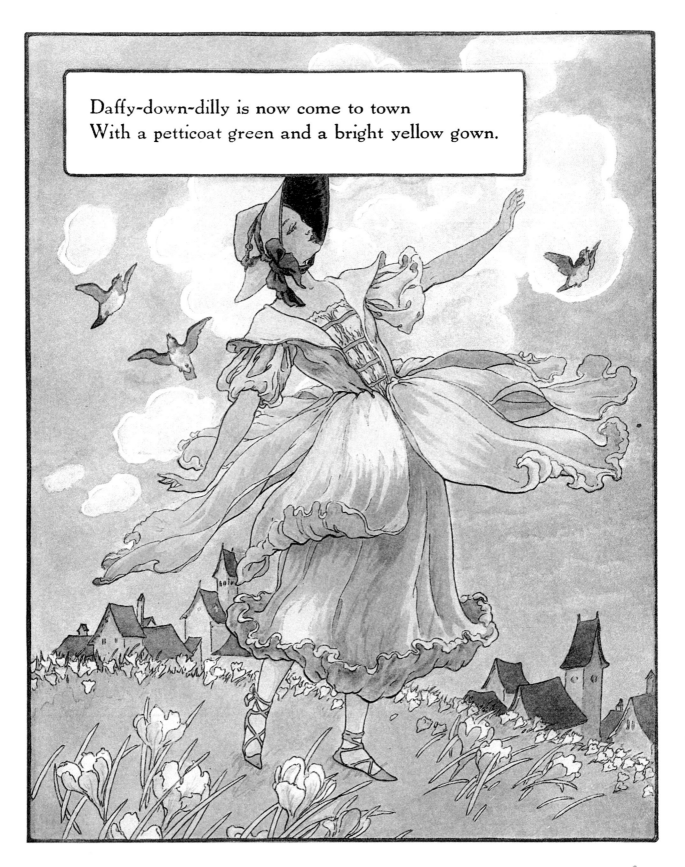

Daffy-down-dilly is now come to town
With a petticoat green and a bright yellow gown.

"Cock, cock, cock, cock,
  I've laid an egg,
   Am I to gang ba-are-foot?"

"Hen, hen, hen, hen,
  I've been up and down
  To every shop in town,
  And cannot find a shoe
  To fit your foot,
   If I'd crow my hea-art out."

The lion and the unicorn
    Were fighting for the crown.
The lion beat the unicorn
    All about the town.
Some gave them white bread,
    And some gave them brown;
Some gave them plum-cake,
    And sent them out of town.

Old King Cole
Was a merry old soul,
And a merry old soul was he;
He called for his pipe,
And he called for his bowl,
And he called for his fiddlers three.

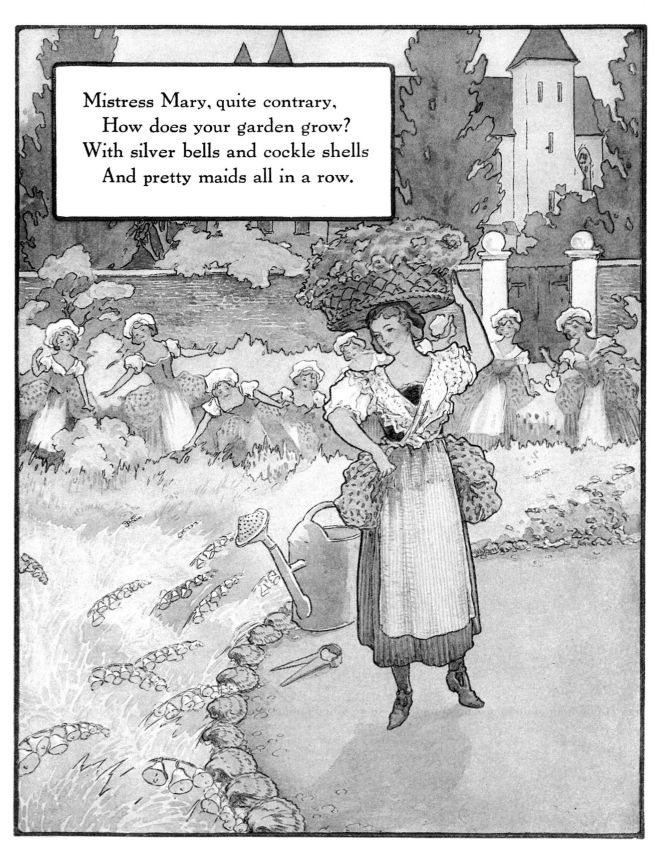

Mistress Mary, quite contrary,
How does your garden grow?
With silver bells and cockle shells
And pretty maids all in a row.

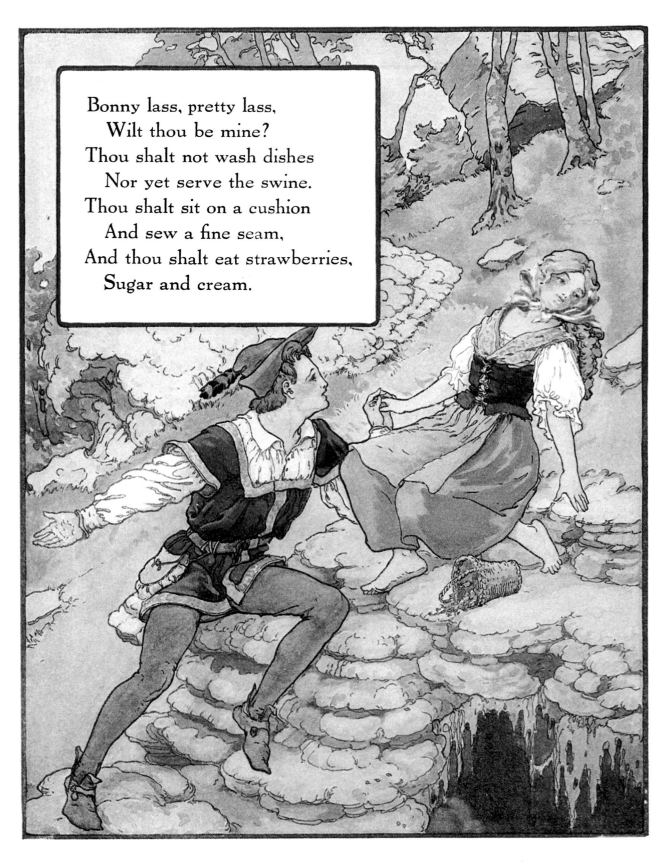

Bonny lass, pretty lass,
　Wilt thou be mine?
Thou shalt not wash dishes
　Nor yet serve the swine.
Thou shalt sit on a cushion
　And sew a fine seam,
And thou shalt eat strawberries,
　Sugar and cream.

Handy-spandy, Jacky dandy,
Loves plum cake and sugar candy.
He bought some at a grocer's shop,
And pleased away went hop, hop, hop.

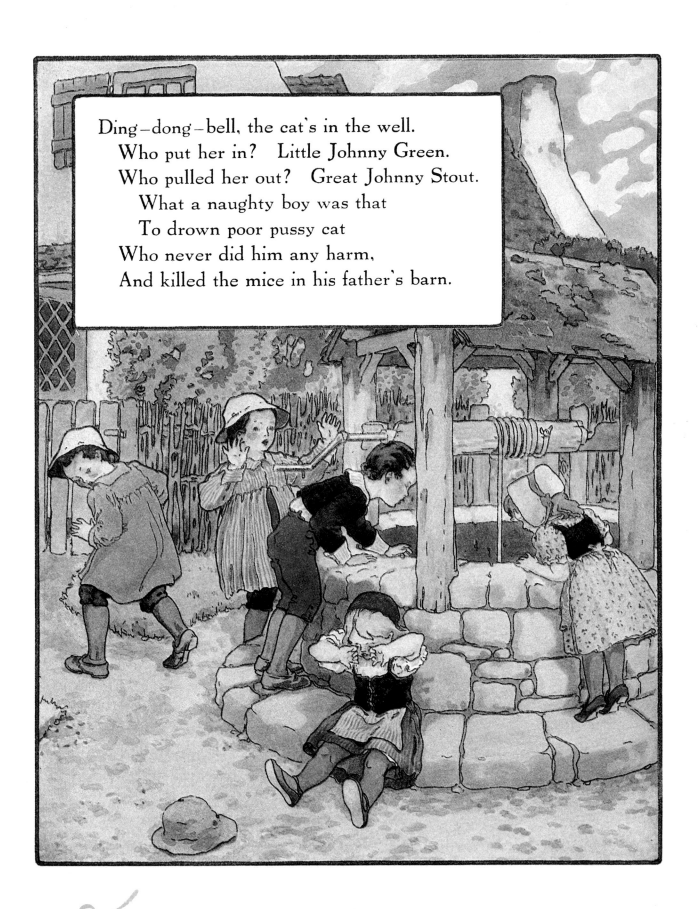

Ding–dong–bell, the cat's in the well.
Who put her in? Little Johnny Green.
Who pulled her out? Great Johnny Stout.
What a naughty boy was that
To drown poor pussy cat
Who never did him any harm,
And killed the mice in his father's barn.

This pig went to market,
That pig stayed at home;
This pig had roast meat,
That pig had none;
This pig went to the barn door,
And cried "week, week," for more.

There were two blackbirds sitting on a hill,
One named Jack and the other named Jill.
Fly away, Jack!   Fly away, Jill!
Come again, Jack!   Come again, Jill!

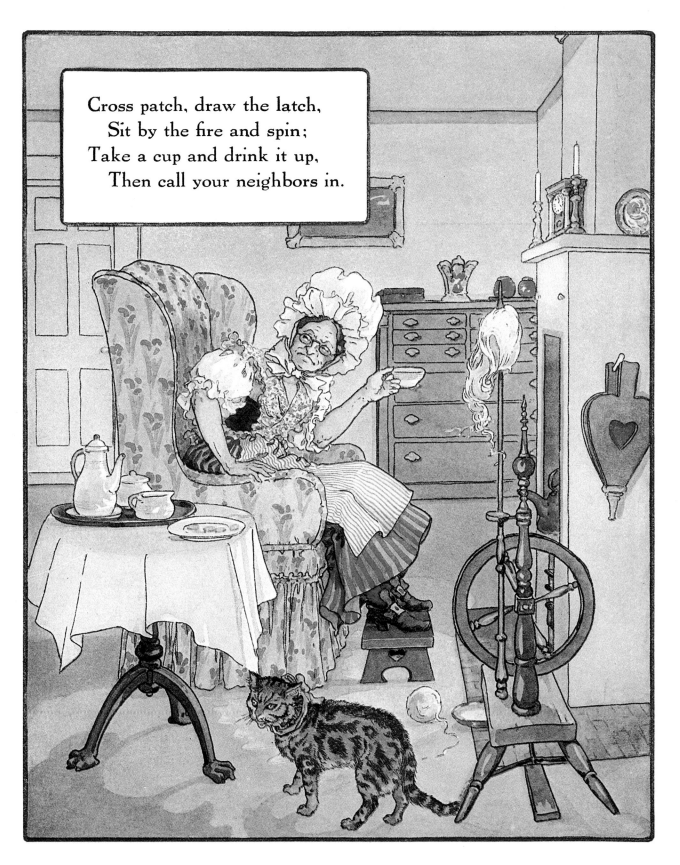

Cross patch, draw the latch,
  Sit by the fire and spin;
Take a cup and drink it up,
  Then call your neighbors in.

Old Mother Hubbard
Went to the cupboard
    To get her poor dog a bone;
But when she came there
The cupboard was bare,
    And so the poor dog had none.

Pease-porridge hot,
Pease-porridge cold,
Pease-porridge in the pot
Nine days old.
Spell me that in four letters;
I will: T H A T.

Polly, put the kettle on,
Polly, put the kettle on,
Polly, put the kettle on,
  We'll all have tea.
Sukey, take it off again,
Sukey, take it off again,
Sukey, take it off again,
  They're all gone away.

The sow came in with the saddle,
The little pig rocked the cradle,
The dish jumped up on the table
To see the pot swallow the ladle.
The spit that stood behind the door
Threw the pudding-stick on the floor.
"Odsplut!", said the gridiron,
    "Can't you agree?
I'm the head constable,
    Bring them to me!"

Little Robin Redbreast sat upon a tree,
Up went the Pussy-Cat, and down went he,
Down came Pussy-Cat, away Robin ran;
Says little Robin Redbreast: "Catch me if you can!"

Little Robin Redbreast jumped upon a spade,
Pussy-Cat jumped after him, and then he was afraid.
Little Robin chirped and sang, and what did Pussy say?
Pussy-Cat said: "Mew, mew, mew," and Robin flew away.

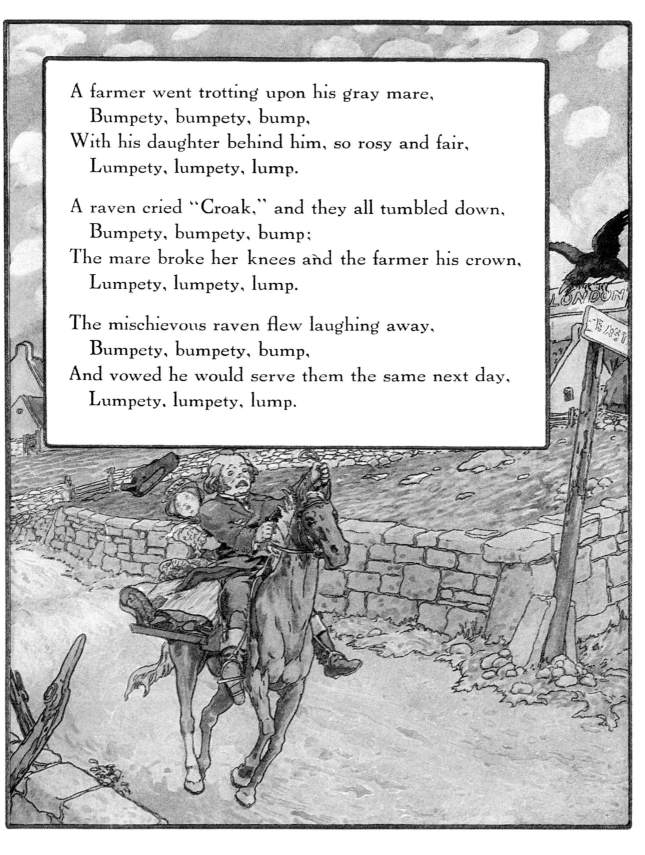

A farmer went trotting upon his gray mare,
    Bumpety, bumpety, bump,
With his daughter behind him, so rosy and fair,
    Lumpety, lumpety, lump.

A raven cried "Croak," and they all tumbled down,
    Bumpety, bumpety, bump;
The mare broke her knees and the farmer his crown,
    Lumpety, lumpety, lump.

The mischievous raven flew laughing away,
    Bumpety, bumpety, bump,
And vowed he would serve them the same next day,
    Lumpety, lumpety, lump.

There was an old woman
  Sold puddings and pies;
She went to the mill,
  And dust flew in her eyes.
While through the streets,
To all she meets
  She ever cries:
  "Hot Pies—Hot Pies."

"Old woman, old woman, shall we go a-shearing?"
"Speak a little louder, sir, I'm very thick o' hearing."
"Old woman, old woman, shall I kiss you dearly?"
"Thank you, kind sir, I hear very clearly."

My little old man and I fell out;
I'll tell you what 'twas all about:
I had money and he had none,
And that's the way the noise begun.

Jack Sprat could eat no fat,
His wife could eat no lean;
So 'twixt them both they cleared the cloth,
And licked the platter clean.

There was an old woman, and what do you think?
She lived upon nothing but victuals and drink;
Victuals and drink were the chief of her diet,
And yet this old woman could never be quiet.

What's the news of the day,
Good neighbor, I pray?
They say the balloon
Has gone up to the moon,

There was a crooked man,
    And he went a crooked mile,
He found a crooked sixpence
    Against a crooked stile;
He bought a crooked cat
    Which caught a crooked mouse,
And they all lived together
    In a little crooked house.

There was a piper had a cow,
    And he had naught to give her;
He pulled out his pipes and played her a tune,
    And bade the cow consider.

The cow considered very well,
    And gave the piper a penny,
And bade him play the other tune,
    "Corn rigs are bonny."

The man in the wilderness
    Asked me
How many strawberries
    Grew in the sea.
I answered him
    As I thought good,
As many red herrings
    As grew in the wood.

Hark!   Hark!
The dogs do bark,
The beggars are coming to town;
Some in rags,
Some in tags,
And some in velvet gown.

As I was going to St. Ives
I met seven wives.
Every wife had seven sacks,
Every sack had seven cats,
Every cat had seven kits.
    Kits, cats, sacks and wives,
    How many were going to St. Ives?

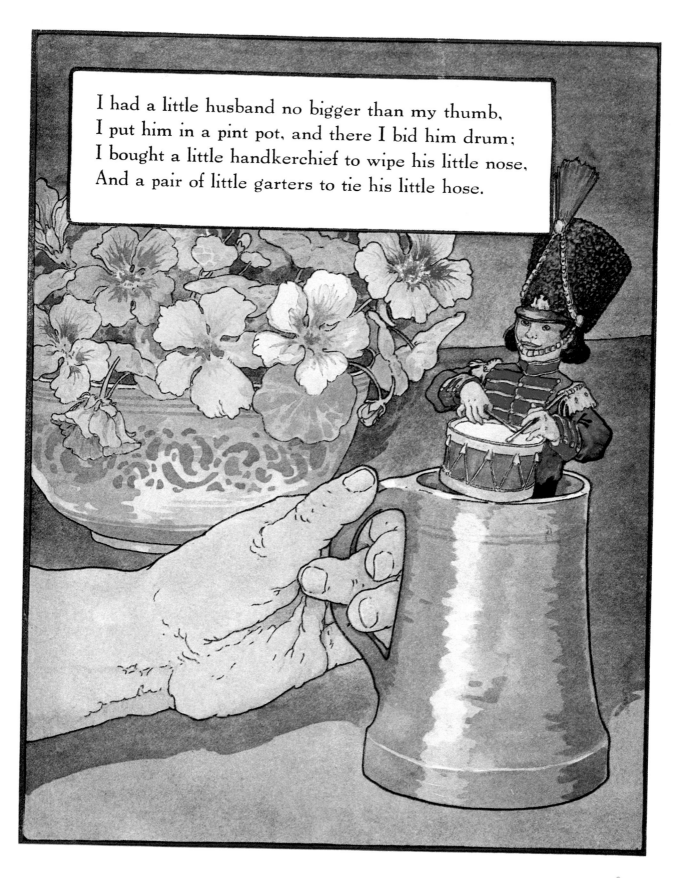

I had a little husband no bigger than my thumb,
I put him in a pint pot, and there I bid him drum:
I bought a little handkerchief to wipe his little nose,
And a pair of little garters to tie his little hose.

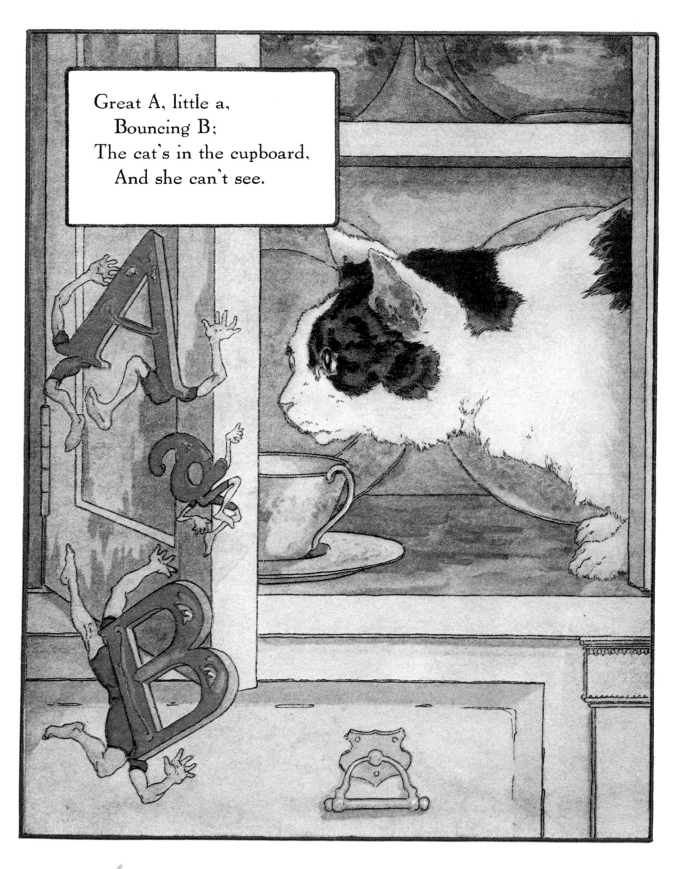

Great A, little a,
   Bouncing B;
The cat's in the cupboard,
   And she can't see.

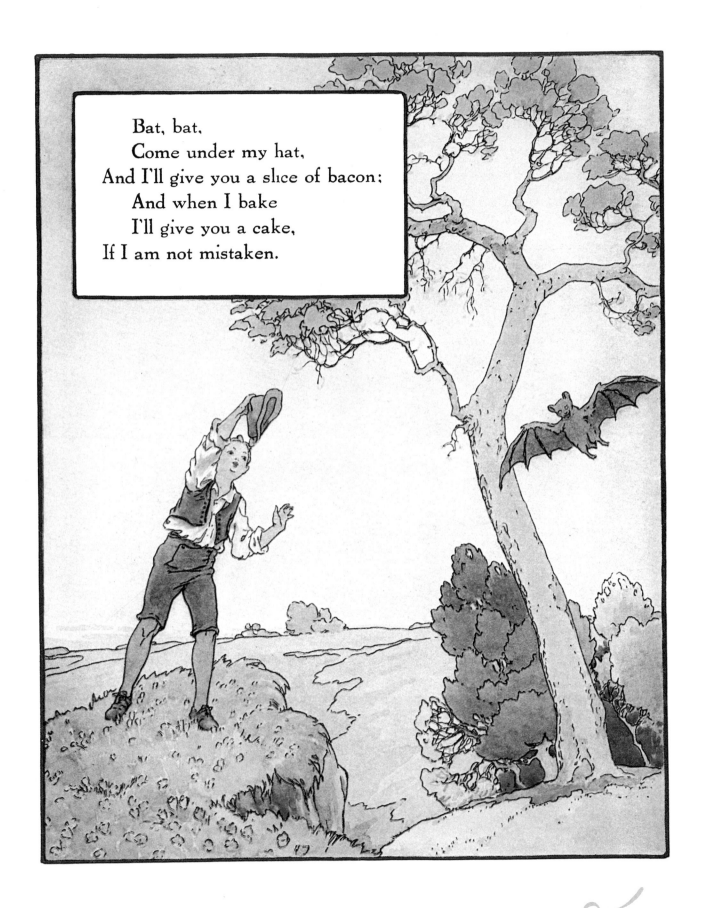

Bat, bat,
Come under my hat,
And I'll give you a slice of bacon;
And when I bake
I'll give you a cake,
If I am not mistaken.

As I was going up Primrose Hill,
  Primrose Hill was dirty;
There I met a pretty lass,
  And she dropped me a curtsey.

Little lass, pretty lass,
  Blessings light upon you;
If I had half-a-crown a day,
  I'd spend it all upon you.

There was a little boy went into a barn
   And lay down on some hay:
A calf came out and smelled about,
   And the little boy ran away.

When good King Arthur ruled his land
  He was a goodly king;
He stole three pecks of barley meal
  To make a bag-pudding.
A bag-pudding the king did make,
  And stuffed it well with plums,
And in it put great lumps of fat
  As big as my two thumbs.
The king and queen did eat thereof,
  And noblemen beside,
And what they could not eat that night
  The queen next morning fried.

"Jacky, come give me your fiddle,
    If ever you mean to thrive."
"Nay, I'll not give my fiddle
    To any man alive.

"If I should give my fiddle
    They'll think that I'm gone mad,
For many a joyful day
    My fiddle and I have had."

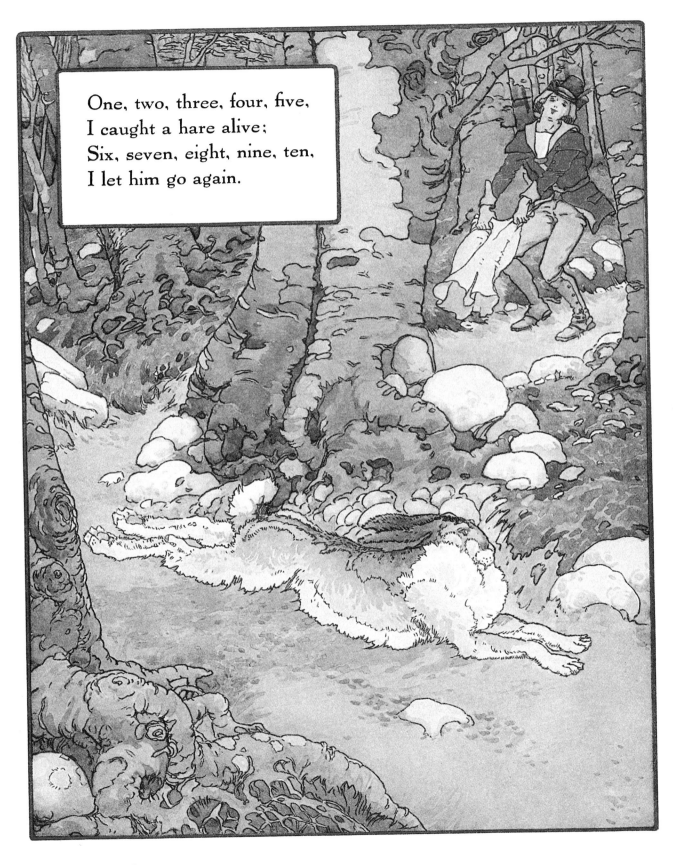

One, two, three, four, five,
I caught a hare alive;
Six, seven, eight, nine, ten,
I let him go again.

The north wind doth blow,
And we shall have snow,
And what will poor robin do then?
                    Poor thing!

He'll sit in the barn
And keep himself warm,
And hide his head under his wing.
                    Poor thing!

"You owe me five shillings,"
  Say the bells of St. Helen's.

"When will you pay me?"
  Say the bells of Old Bailey.

"When I grow rich,"
  Say the bells of Shoreditch.

"When will that be?"
  Say the bells of Stepney.

"I do not know,"
  Says the great Bell of Bow.

"Two sticks in an apple,"
  Ring the bells of Whitechapel.

"Halfpence and farthings,"
  Say the bells of St. Martin's.

"Kettles and pans,"
  Say the bells of St. Ann's.

"Brickbats and tiles,"
  Say the bells of St. Giles.

"Old shoes and slippers,"
  Say the bells of St. Peter's.

"Pokers and tongs,"
  Say the bells of St. John's.

There was a man in our town,
    And he was wondrous wise,
He jumped into a bramble-bush,
    And scratched out both his eyes;
And when he saw his eyes were out,
    With all his might and main
He jumped into another bush
    And scratched them in again.

INDEX

(ARRANGED IN ORDER OF APPEARANCE)